all the broken pieces

A NOVEL IN VERSE BY **ann e. burg**

SCHOLASTIC INC.
NEW YORK TORONTO LONDON AUCKLAND
SYDNEY MEXICO CITY NEW DELHI HONG KONG

ISBN: 978-0-545-23502-0

12 11 10 9 8 7 6 5 4 3 2 1   10 11 12 13 14 15/0

Printed in the U.S.A.   40

First Scholastic paperback printing, January 2010

The display type was set in American Typewriter Bold, P22Cage Extras, and Copperplate Bold. The text type was set in 12-pt. Baskerville Regular. Book design by Marijka Kostiw

For my brothers,

Joseph & Michael

My name is Matt Pin
and her name, I remember,
is Phang My.
His name
I will never say,
though forever I carry his blood
in my blood,
forever his bones
stretch in my bones.
To me,
he is nothing.
If he stumbled on me now,
I wonder,
would he see himself in my eyes?
And I?
Would I recognize the dragon
who went beyond the mountain
and never came back?

I carry her too,
her blood in my blood,
her bones in my bones.
Eyes I will not forget,
though I see them
only in dreams,
in fog,
through thick clouds of smoke.
I hear her voice,
thin, shrill staccato notes,
her words short puffs of air
that push me along,
inch by inch, breath by breath.
In choking mist
and wailing dust,
through sounds
of whirring helicopters
and open prayers,
I hear her.
You cannot stay here,
she says.
Here you will be like dust.
Bui Doi.
Dust of life.
You cannot stay here.

≡

I remember little,
but I remember.

There were babies crying
and mothers screaming,
begging soldiers to take
their children.

Take her, take him.
Please let them live!

Pushing, praying, pleading.

I would rather be dust
on the road
than leave *her*.

But it is not enough.
She pushes me forward,
through screaming madness
and choking dust,
through fear and fog,
through smoke and death,
through whirring sounds

4   of helicopter prayers,
and night falling like
rain-soaked stars.

Survive,
she says.
Remember
not this shame.

☰

My father says
when I am older,
there are places I can go
to find him,
but I won't.

What good would it do?

He never saw my face.
But she was already swelled
with love for him when he left,
taking with him
his blue-eyed promise
that it would not end there,
with the smell of burnt flesh
and the sound of crying children.

I will come back,
you said,
and she believed you.

Why not?

You shared her home,
she called you husband,
why should she not believe you?

6   But you did *not* come back.

What is there left to say?

Why should I find you?

≡

The house I live in now
is big,
but its walls are thin.
At night, when they
think I am asleep,
I hear the news on TV.
I hear them talk.

It's no wonder
the soldiers are broken,
Dad says.
When they left, they were
high school heroes,
stars of the football team,
with pretty girlfriends.
Now look at them—
hobbling on crutches,
rolling themselves
in wheelchairs,
while people throw things—

tomatoes,
rotten apples,

angry words

≡

I have a now brother.
He doesn't look like me.
I'm too much fall—
wet brown leaves
under a darkening sky.
Tommy is summer—
sunlight, peaches,
wide, grinning sky.
Even Tommy's hair is summer.
Curls cling to his scalp like
the yellow-and-white sweet corn
at McGreavy's Market.
Only one straight tuft sticks up,
like a clump of sun-scorched hay.

≡

I have another brother.
Dark skin, dark eyes,
straight black hair,
and a laugh like a
babbling, bubbling,
quickly tumbling
brook.

She would not let him come.

If we got separated,
he might not survive.

Who would want a little boy
mangled and deformed,
she said,
with missing fingers
and stumps instead of legs?
Who would want a little boy
like that?

I would, I begged.

But *no,* she said.
You are strong, she said.
You go.

10 *When you are grown,*
if you still remember,
you can come back.

How can I go back?
Where would I look?
What would I say?

If I remember.
How can I forget?

☰

My now mother
is small like me.
Her hair is long
and yellow.
She fills my room
with the smell
of summer.

When I wake
in the middle of the night
full of screams
and flashes,
she sits on the edge
of my bed,
her pale hands move
gently across my face.

Her voice is soft,
like warm honey.
She sings a quiet song.

There is darkness on the water.
There is darkness on the land.
There is darkness all around us,
but I will hold your hand.

You are safe, my precious child.
You are safe now, you are home.
We have found you and we love you.
You will never be alone.

There are no mines here,
no flames, no screams,
no sounds of helicopters
or shouting guns.

I am safe.

How can I
be home?

≡

My father
has chestnut-colored eyes
and short brown hair
that is starting
to wear away in front.
His well-scrubbed hands
are square and strong.

Every Saturday afternoon,
if it is not too cold
or rainy,
we go to the park.

My father and I
toss a ball.

I catch it
in my oversized glove.

Again and again,

he pitches,
I catch.

I pitch,
he catches.

14   Back and forth,
        back and forth,
        until dusk creeps in
        and the ball
        is just a swiftly
        moving shadow
        fading into darkness.

        ≡

Every time at the park,
I remember the first time.

What is this place? I thought.
I was small.
Small, but not young.
I was almost ten,
but I looked much younger
than the other boys my age.

There were two boys
on a swing
and a little girl
bouncing
on a pink elephant
with gray spots.

There was a painted
ladybug seesaw,
a shiny slide,
and monkey bars.

Even now,
sometimes
I cannot believe it.
I cannot believe

so different a place.
A place made
just for children.

I think about him.
I wonder where he is.

He would like it here.

≡

Tommy is too young
to play ball.
When he comes
to the park,
we put him
on the swing.
Higher, he says,
and I pull him
back as far
as I can reach
and then let go.
Higher, he says,
laughing.
His small fists
squeeze the chain.
His perfect toes
dangle
inside
bright red sneakers.

In school
for Veterans Day
we write essays
on freedom.
I write,

18

Freedom is the color
of bright red sneakers.

What is this? the teacher asks.
Does this make sense?

≡

The first two years,
I went back to the
adoption agency
every Saturday morning
to learn English.

Once a month,
my mother and father
came with me.
We spent
the day reading
legends and fairy tales,
how Au Co was
a beautiful mountain fairy
who married
Lac Long Quan,
a daring dragon prince.
We celebrated Tet
and Tet Trung Thu.
We ate *banh giay*
and played *danh phet*.

We did not talk about
the American War,
how tanks lumbered

in the roads
like drunken elephants,
and bombs fell
from the sky
like dead crows.

≡

For two years,
I learned about Vietnam,
but it wasn't any
Vietnam I remembered.

The teacher
was a tiny woman
with small eyes
who always stayed
in one spot
when she talked,
but whose words rolled
up and down,
up and down
the classroom walls
like a glass marble.

She told happy stories
of people and places
I did not know.

Colorful costumes
and carnival dragons
live in another Vietnam,
a Vietnam
that I do not remember.

≡

I close my eyes.
I listen.

I try to remember
the colors,

but I cannot.

I try to form
dragons from
dust,

but I cannot.

I try again.
But I cannot.

My Vietnam
is drenched
in smoke and fog.

It has no parks
or playgrounds,
no classrooms
or teachers.

It is not
on any map
or in any book.

My Vietnam is
only
a pocketful
of broken pieces
I carry
inside me.

≡

The children in that class
look at me strangely.
My lashes are not flat
and straight like theirs.
Their hair is not thick
and brown like mine.

We are all children
born in Vietnam.

Most of us
have two names.

A new name
to welcome us,
and an old name
to remind us.

Still, I am different.

My face
is part American.

But anyway,
twice a year

we get together.
We celebrate
Tet or Tet Trung Thu.

These customs
are strange to me,
but still
my stomach aches
with sadness.

I want to go back.

≡

The agency classroom
is decorated with
red and gold streamers.
There are fresh fruits,
flowers, and sticky
little rice cakes
on the teacher's desk.

Are you all right?
my mother asks.
She feels my forehead.
She touches my face.
She compliments my
paper dragon and my
folded lantern.

I shrug.
I'm just not hungry.
I give her my dragon
and my lantern.
Here, these are for you.

*Maybe he's getting too
old for all this,*
my father says.

He needs to experience
his culture,
my mother answers.

At night,
when I try to sleep,
I hear her cry.

≡

Music is soothing.

My mother's words
float through
the thin walls.

Maybe music will help
soothe his monsters.

Let him play baseball,
my father answers.
He has a good arm.

I turn out the light
and keep listening,
but it's quiet now,

darkness on the water,
darkness on the land.

≡

In the day,
Jeff Harding works at
the same hospital
as my father.

At night,
he teaches piano.

Jeff was supposed
to go to a school
for music,
a special school
in New York City.

Instead,
he went to Vietnam.

He rode the
helicopter ambulances
that rescued
the wounded.
He took care of them,
right there
on the helicopter.

Maybe one day
Jeff can show you
his Dustoff patch,
Dad says
Saturday during breakfast.

But I know he won't.

Jeff's Vietnam
is my Vietnam,

the Vietnam nobody talks about
on Saturday mornings.

≡

On Wednesdays,
an hour
before dinner,
I sit at the piano.
My fingers stretch
across the keys
like a soundless
spider.

Jeff stands
beside the bench
as I play.
He crosses his arms
and smiles.
You can hit the keys a
little harder, he says.

Let's look at the notations.
He points to the fancy S.
That's the treble clef.
Each line and space is lettered
so we'll know what note to play.
Let's learn the lines first.
Here's a way to remember them.

He puts his foot up
on the bench
and taps each line
with a pencil.
Every good boy deserves fudge.
He smiles and
taps them again.
Every good boy does fine.

≡

The next day,
after school,
I practice piano
for half an hour.

Some kids complain
about practicing piano,
but not me.
Notes are like numbers,
never changing.
Staccato or sustained,
pounded or tapped,
notes always stay
the same.

Ten divided by two
will always be five.

Every good boy
will always do fine.

I like that.

≡

That night,
when Dad comes home
from work,
we practice baseball
in the backyard.

For the past two years,
we've gone
to the rec field
to watch the kids
pitching, hitting,
running bases.

They are my age
but bigger.

Every year, Dad says,
You have a good arm, Matt.
You should try out.

Maybe next year,
I always say.

You have a good arm, Matt,
Dad says as

a high ball crackles
through the branches
in a darkening sky.
*You should try out
for the school team.*

≡

Outside the school gym,
the sign-up sheet shows
forty kids.
Forty kids
pitching,
hitting,
running
for fourteen spots
on the team.

This year,
I surprise him.
One of those names
is mine.

≡

Open practice
before tryouts
is every day this week
from three until four-thirty.
Tommy and my mother
pick me up
in the Impala.
I throw my stuff
in the backseat.
Tommy climbs on my lap,
babbles,
and pulls my ears
the whole way home.

Leave Matt alone,
my mother says.
She shakes her head
and smiles at me.
Her hair moves
like sunshine.
He misses you
when you're at school.

At home,
I quickly shower
and practice my scales
before Jeff comes.

One–two–three–*under*,
one–two–three–
four–five.
Five–four–three–
two–one–
over–three—ugh!

Why do I always stumble
going back?

≡

At the door,
Jeff and my mother talk.
Tommy plays with the pots
in the kitchen.
My fingers tap the air
while I wait.

Go ahead, Jeff finally says.
Let's get started.

Every week, I nod and say,
Okay, and every week, I wait.
Even with Tommy's clatter,
I don't want to disturb them.

≡

My fingers stumble
through the scales
and through
"The Gypsy Camp."

They crowd the keys,
landing in two spots
at the same time.
They slip, clank, and clash
into sounds
that aren't music.

Watch, Jeff says calmly
when my fingers freeze
in frustration.

Jeff's fingers are
bigger than mine,
but they know how
to touch each key,
one at a time.
They unlock each sound
separately.

Jeff doesn't make mistakes.

His fingers brush
across the piano keys
like branches
of the tamarind
swaying in the wind.
How can such big hands
make such quiet music?

≡

*I've been practicing
a lot longer
than you,* he says.
Slow down. Be patient.

I wish I could be.
Jeff is slow, patient,
quiet.
But he isn't
an afraid quiet.
Just a calm quiet,
like he's looked into
a closet of monsters
and found empty
candy wrappers instead.

I wish I
could do that.

≡

*It's great being part
of a team,* Dad says.

Tommy's upstairs
taking his bath
and the two of us
are clearing the table.

*It's great being
part of something
bigger than yourself.*

*I might not make it, Dad.
Forty kids are trying out.
I might get cut.*

I don't see how, Dad says.
*You've got a great arm.
Coach Robeson's a great coach.
He won't let you get away.*

≡

Tryouts
are on Monday.

On Tuesday,
we'll learn
who made the team.

On Wednesday,
fourteen of us
will learn our positions.

The rest of us
will creep home
with our caps
pulled down tight,
slanted way below our noses
so no one can see us cry.

≡

I have my cap.
I have my
hooded sweatshirt.
I'm ready.

But whether I
make the team
or not,
I won't cry.

All my tears
I left
in Vietnam.

≡

Tryouts start
just like training.
We stretch.
We run.
Coach Louis,
the assistant coach,
hits ground balls.

But the air is jumpy.
Electric currents spark
the gym.

Coach Robeson
is walking around
with a clipboard,
smiling, nodding,
scratching notes
and names.

At first I thought
I heard wrong.
I never bothered
anyone.
Why would anyone
bother me?
But when different kids
get called to bat,
and I'm told to stay
and pitch,
their voices
get stronger.

Someone steps in to bat,
Coach Robeson and Coach Louis
huddle,
and the words hit me
like a punch.

Billy Alden is the loudest.
Hey, Frog-face,
where'd you learn
to play baseball,
in a rice paddy?

Davey Laice grumbles,
Matt-the-rat,
if you make the team,
I'll quit.

When tryouts
are over,
Rob Brennan
bumps into me.
I fall
into the bleachers.
When I stand up again,
he hisses
in my ear,
My brother died
because of you.

≡

If I drop out now,
my father
will ask questions.
If I tell anyone,
I *will* be a rat.

Last year Billy
accidentally
dumped sour milk
on a fifth grader
who wouldn't give him
one of his Twinkies.
Everyone still calls the kid
"stink."

Who knows what
will happen to me?

I pull my cap down tight
and pray I get cut.

≡

Dad meets me outside the gym
after tryouts.

How'd it go?

Okay.

I bet it went better than that.
He puts his arm
around my shoulder
and we walk to the car.

When he turns the key,
the radio goes on with the motor.
Right away, the Bee Gees
start singing,
Got the wings of heaven
on my shoes.
I wish I did. I'd fly far away
from Billy and Davey and Rob.

Dad starts singing
with the radio.
His voice is low and off-key.

Whether you're a brother
or whether you're a mother,
You're stayin' alive, stayin' alive,
he sings quietly,
bopping his head
and his shoulders.
Feel the city breakin' and everybody shakin',
'cause we're stayin' alive, stayin' alive.
Ha, ha, ha, stayin' alive, stayin' alive.

It's hard to worry about stuff
when my father sings.

Don't worry, he says,
nodding his head to the music.
You've got a great arm.
You'll make the team.

He pushes up my hat and smiles.
Even if you don't make it,
you'll always be our MVP.

Whether you're a brother
or whether you're a mother,
you'll always be our MVP.

≡

I'm trying to read *Kidnapped*
but the Bee Gees are rolling
through my head.

Stayin' alive,
stayin' alive.

They rock and roll
through my head
as I wash up for dinner,

as I chew my meat loaf
and my mashed potatoes.

Stayin' alive,
stayin' alive.

As Tommy bangs
on his high chair
and squashes
his sliced bananas,

as my mother offers
stayin' alime
Jell-O for dessert.

Stayin' alive,
stayin' alive.

Whether you're a mother
or whether you're a brother,

my brother died
because of you.

≡

On Wednesday
the list is posted
outside the gym.
I check it twice.

My stomach drops.

Only four seventh graders
made the team,
and I am one of them.

There's a note
taped to my locker.
It's a picture
of a rice field
torn from
a magazine.

In black marker someone
drew a big-eyed rat
and wrote the words
Matt-the-rat.

I know what the note means.

*Because of you
there's no place for me.*

Prejudice is ignorance
in a catcher's mask,
Coach Robeson says, coughing.
His face is white-angry
and his eyes
are like steel bullets.
I didn't tell anyone
about the note
but somehow Coach
must have found out.

Alex, Billy, and Rob
are the only other seventh graders
who made the team.

Alex is a quiet boy
with curly hair and glasses
who lives across the street from me.
Sometimes we ride our bikes
together or toss the ball around.
Did he know about the note?
Did he tell Coach Robeson?

There are two Michaels, a Drew,
an Eric, a Daniel, and a few boys

I don't even know yet.
Did they know about the note?
Would they even care?

I hear one more derogatory comment,
Coach says, looking at everyone
slow and steady,
one at a time,
his sharp eyes
locking their eyes
before they have a chance
to look down,
you won't play on any team,
in any school, in any town.
Period.
Either plan to play like a team,
or get out
now.

He doesn't mention my name
or the note.

Sometimes the words people don't say
are as powerful as the ones they do.

≡

Most of the time
I pitch,
but sometimes
I play shortstop.

Standing between
second and third
is tricky.
Do I shift toward second,
or lean toward third?
Do I trust
that my teammate
wants to win
more than he wants
to hurt me?

I'd rather pitch.

It's just me
and the ball
and the batter.
Me and my arm
and my eyes.

I face my enemy head-on,
and he's always on the other team.

≡

The assignment is
easy enough.

Without describing them physically,
choose one member of your family,
and write a brief character sketch
about them. Remember, we learn
more about a character
through their actions than their appearance.
Actions speak louder than adjectives.

I pull a pencil
from my top drawer.

My top drawer
is full of pencils, new,
used, half used, and
all-the-way-to-the-eraser-cap used.
I never get rid of pencils.
I never get rid of anything.
Who knows?
Even a stub
is worth something.

If bombs fall here,
if something so terrible
ever happens
that I get sent away,
I'll stuff everything
I can fit
into my pockets.

Even the broken pieces
are worth something
to me.

≡

I pull out a well-sharpened pencil
with a high, clean eraser.

My mother, I write.
I draw a box around the word *My*
and another box
around the word *mother.*
I color the boxes lightly.
I can still read the words so
I keep coloring them.

Darker and darker.

And darker.

Soon I have just one
long rectangle.

Just a plain,
dark,
black
box.

No one would even know
there's something inside.

≡

The piano sits
in an alcove
at the bottom
of the stairs,
between the den
and the kitchen,
closer to the den
but in a separate
space.

It's hard not
to touch the keys
as I pass by.

When I wait
for my mother
to pack a snack
for Tommy, or
when the phone
rings just as we're
leaving the house,
I pull out the bench,
and zip through the C scale
or "Shenandoah"'s
rolling river.

62

When I play the piano,
I'm sheltered
in that safe place
where the only thing
that matters
is music.

☰

Something's going on.
They're disagreeing
about something.

I hear whispering as I pass
their bedroom door.

I wait. I listen.

It might be better for everyone,
she says.

*I'm just not convinced
it's a good idea,* he answers.

*But maybe we can't provide
what he needs, Michael.
Mrs. Mack called yesterday.
Matt's classwork is slipping.
He's not doing his homework.
Maybe if he goes, he'll understand more.*

*He's just a boy. How much more
can he understand?*

I hear them move toward the door
and I jump.

At the top of the stairs,
she smiles at me,
smiles like my teammates,
like she was just talking about
what color to paint the hallway,
or whether we should have potatoes
or rice for dinner.

Time to wash for supper, Matt,
she says.

I feel something like a cold fish
shimmy inside me.

Maybe it's time
to let me go.
Now they have Tommy,
happy as summer,
and even starting to say,
Me play ball.

With a cute kid like him,
why do they need me?

≡

If I run away,
maybe they'll miss me
and want me back.

But where would I go?
And what about Tommy?
Who would he follow around,
saying, *Ball, ball, play ball?*

In the yard, I want to run,
but my legs are locked.
It is late afternoon.
The sun still shines bright.
My mother watches
from the window.
Her face is in the shadows.
Her hair and her eyes
seem darker than they are.
She studies me.
Her smile
is forced and sad.

My feet are heavy as mud.

≡

That night, after dinner,
Dad and I clear the dishes
while Tommy takes his bath.
Then Dad sits in the kitchen
and reads the paper.
I go in the den
and watch TV.

But it's not a good
TV night
so I lie on the couch
and think instead.

≡

My parents say they love me.
He says
I'll always be his MVP.
She says
I'm safe, I'm home.

But what about
my mother in Vietnam?
Didn't she say
she loved me too?
And didn't he say
that he loved her?
And didn't he leave
and never come back?
And didn't she
give me away?
And didn't I love him
even though
his hands and legs
were mangled stumps?
And didn't I leave anyway?

Maybe love is like
a monsoon rain.
When it rains
really hard and heavy,

it seems like
it will never end
and we'll swim in mud
forever.

But then the wind shifts,
and the earth grows
dry and cracked.
Every gurgle and ooze
tiptoes away
and we're left wishing
and waiting
for rain again.

Maybe love is like that.
Maybe the wind shifts
and love just tiptoes away.

≡

I'm going to study more.
I'm going to practice
the piano more.
Maybe if I get all A's
and master the B major scale,
if I pitch better,
if I keep my room neater,
and take out the garbage,
and clean the garage,
if I pick up Tommy's bus people
and farm animals,
and teach him
how to write his name,

maybe then they'll keep me.

At least I think they'll keep me
until the end of baseball season.

My father likes baseball
too much to let me go
before the season's over.

≡

Partner up and start throwing,
Coach says when I get to the field
on the day of our first game.

I partner up with Alex, as usual.

If he minds being partnered
with me, he never says so.
He just pushes up his glasses,
nods, and starts tossing the ball.
My arm feels good.
Loose and powerful.

Arms are stretching,
balls are flying,
mounds of dirt
are kicked and spit on.

Finally the whistle blows.
We're ready.

The game between
the Lynbrook Lions
and the Plymouth Pirates—
our biggest rivals—
is about to begin.

≡

The top of the inning
is perfect.
Michael V. gets a base hit
on the first pitch.
Rob's the next batter up.
The first ball whizzes by him
for a strike.
The next ball follows
the same path,
but this time
Rob is ready.
He pulls back
and swings hard.
The ball bounds deep
into left field
for a double.

Billy strikes out,
and so does Michael L.,
but Daniel's home run
drives in the runners
on second and third.
Three runs for the Lions!
Alex gets out on a fly,
but it doesn't matter.
The Lynbrook Lions
are roaring.

≡

We take the field.

The first batter
is a round boy
with short legs
who looks like
he'll be a slow runner.
I take a deep breath
and sneak a look
at Coach Robeson.
His nod pushes down
the butterflies
in my stomach.

I twist the ball
in my glove,
pull back my right arm,
and let the ball fly.

It takes off
like it has wings,
and then, just as it reaches
home plate, it drops.

Strike one, the umpire signals.

I pull my hat down,
look around,
and let go another sinker.

Strike two.

I always feel power
in my arm,
but sometimes between
the windup and the release
there is time enough
for something else,
for the smallest
flick of my wrist.

These pitches
sail through the air
and drop at the batter's feet
like a wounded bird.

Strike three.

The boy with the short legs
shakes his head
and kicks the dirt.

The second batter
approaches the batter's box.
I feel my shoulders tense.
This kid should play football
instead of baseball.

Coach Robeson nods again.

I take a deep breath
and twist the ball in my glove.
I kick my leg up,
rock my arm back,
and hurl the ball forward.

It looks like a perfect
home run pitch, but just
when the ball and bat
should make contact,
the ball falls,
and the bat slices the air.

Strike one.

I do it again.

And again.

Strike three.

The third batter is stiff.
He doesn't move his head
or blink his eyes.
He swings at
the first three pitches
even though the second is low,
and the third is wild.

In less than five minutes,
the Lions have pounded
the Pirates to dust.

≡

Just keep doing what you're doing,
Coach Robeson says to me.

Coach Louis pats me
on the back and smiles.
Great job, Matt.

Wow, Michael V. says,
that was unbelievable.

They didn't even get one hit,
Alex says.

Billy glares,
then turns away.

Rob doesn't say a word
either.

Not even after
the second inning
or the third.

Not even when
I strike out
the final batter,

or when people
from both sides
of the bleachers
cheer wildly for me,
and we crush
the Pirates
11–0.

≡

After the game,
everyone goes to
Rosie O's Pizza Planet
to celebrate.

Everyone is talking
at once.

What a game!

Did you see the look
on number five's face?
He's their star player.

My father is glowing.

My mother has hung
her purple-blue shawl
from a wooden peg
and is busy handing out
slices of pizza.

Tommy is with our
neighbor Mrs. Pennotti.

I look over at Rob.

He's breaking his crust
into little pieces and
leaving it on the plate,
not talking to anyone.

≡

On Wednesday,
I sit at the piano
and play for Jeff.
*Isn't that supposed to be
a lonesome ballad?*
my mother asks.
She's on her way
upstairs, but stops
and puts down
her blue plastic
laundry basket.

Jeff smiles at me.
*It's hard to play slow
and full of sorrow
when you've pitched
a perfect game.*

I smile too.
At least Jeff knows
there's something
I do well.

Coach Robeson starts
the next practice
by reminding us
what we're capable of
when we work
together.

It's all about teamwork,
he says.
He coughs into his sleeve,
then looks at me
and smiles.

Matt was focused.
He did a great job.
But you all did.
You all worked
together.
That's what makes
a championship team.
Working together.

After that,
it's practice as usual.
Some stretching.

Some bunting.
Some base-running drills.

When we are
getting ready to leave,
Rob stops
to tie his sneaker
right where
I'm standing.
He gets up with his back
to Coach Robeson.

Proud of yourself, Ace?
he hisses quietly.
Hey, even a Frog-face
can get lucky, I guess.

≡

On Saturday, my parents
have to go to a funeral.
The father of one of
the hospital nurses
Dad works with died.

I'm on my stomach,
trying to get a stuffed
elephant that Tommy
has wedged between
the wall and the piano.

I hear my father
and my mother
talking in the kitchen.

He lived a good life,
Dad says.
I'm sure he's at peace.

I wonder what happens
to people if they don't
live a good life,
if they do something terrible.

Do they ever find peace?

Mrs. Pennotti is going
to watch Tommy.
Jeff will bring me
to the game
and take me to lunch
afterward.

It's a good thing
I'm not pitching.

How can I focus
on pitching when
I'm riding in Jeff's
silver Corvette?

≡

We beat the Titans 5–2
even though I bobbled a hit
and cost us a run.

My knees were bent,
my eyes on the batter.
The ball landed
safe inside my glove,
but then—
I looked back
to make sure
Jeff was watching
—I fumbled.
I dropped the ball
and by the time
I picked it up
and threw it,
the runner on third
had advanced home.

When we walk
back to the dugout
at the end of the inning,
Rob whispers,
What's the matter, Frog-face?
Lose your focus?

≡

Chrome wheels
and leather seats
don't cheer me.
A burger
and french fries
don't cheer me.
I'm slumped
in our booth
at the diner
rearranging
my food.

Hey, even Ron Guidry
makes mistakes,
Jeff says as he opens
the bottle of ketchup
and squeezes some
onto his open hamburger.

He stares at the thick
red blob a long time,
like he's trying to make
sense of something,
like somehow
the splattered ketchup
holds the key.

≡

Matt, he finally says,
I'd like to talk to you
about Vietnam.

Fear shivers
down my spine,
a silver shot
that explodes
inside me,

shattering everything

and right there
in that moment,

rain,
like a thousand
scattered bullets,
bounces
around me.

≡

I'm running in the mud,
running but not moving,
and I can scarcely
breathe for the pellets of
rain spraying *everywhere*.

I hear him scream
when he steps
where he should not step.
I shout his name.
I push through the rain
and make my way over
to where he lies.
I lift him
and carry him home,
falling deeper and deeper
into heavy, thick mud
that sticks to my skin,
and weighs me down,
and makes him
so heavy
even though
I carried him
on my back
so easily
just yesterday.

≡

I carry my brother's
bruised and wailing body
in my arms

and all the colors—

the green paddies
and the pink lotus,
the blue sky
and the silver moon—

wash into a red mud.

And she's there too,
her eyes closed,
cradling him,
telling me
it isn't my fault,

it isn't me
who leaves traps
for small children

or rains down bombs
that fall like dead crows.

≡

It's not your fault,

she repeats,
holding him in one arm
and me in the other

holding me
and rocking me.

It's not your fault.

You're safe, Matt.
You're safe.

It's going to be okay.

There is darkness all around us,
but you will never be alone.

≡

His voice is gentle
and low
like a lullaby.
His arms are around
my shaking shoulders,
his chant so steady and soft
that my heart gradually
calms,
and I breathe deeply
and slowly.

What's
happened?

Jeff is sitting
on my side of the booth.

The afternoon sunlight
washes through me.

Her voice
fades to a whisper,

and all I want to do
is sleep.

≡

My mother and father are home
when we get back,
but Tommy is not.

I wonder where he is.

How was the game? my father asks.
We are barely
through the door.
I just shrug.
Matt played great, Jeff lies.
They won again.

Dad beams.
Later, would Jeff tell him
the truth? Would he tell
him I dropped the ball,
that I started shivering
at the diner,
shivering and shaking
for no reason at all?

I thought I'd ask him,
Jeff says, *but he got upset.*

Ask me what?

My father's look
jumps across the space
between us as if he's
scooping me into his arms.
Let's go into the kitchen.

My mother looks
at my father
and then at me.
She takes a deep breath.
*Okay, let's get everything
out in the open,* she says.

So this is it.
That's why Tommy's not here.

My head hurts.
I feel dizzy
and so tired
I could sleep forever.

≡

Sit down, Matt,
we've been meaning to talk to you,
she says.

I sit down.
I concentrate on the table,
studying the lines
in the wood,
how some rings are thin
and perfect
like they were painted by an artist,
and some are thick and jagged,
shaped like little sideways mountains.
I've sat at this table
so many times
but never noticed
the sideways mountains before.
I wonder how long it takes
to get placed in foster care.
I wonder how many more
lime Jell-Os I'll have.
How many more piggyback rides
I'll give Tommy.
How many nights at my desk?
How many nights asleep
in my own bed?

≡

Last year, there was a foster kid
in our class. His name was Troy.
On the first day of school,
a quarter popped out of Troy's pocket
and rolled under the radiator.
When Troy knelt down to get it,
I saw the soles of his sneakers.
They were so smooth
they looked transparent.

Jeff is talking,
I can hear his voice,
but his words don't make sense.
The rolling quarter
is causing some kind
of silver interference,
like a flattened bullet
in my brain.
I wonder what makes
some rings in the wood perfect
and others like jagged scars.

If I go into foster care,
I wonder,
will I get to keep my sneakers?

≡

My mother talks
slowly and gently.
Her fluttery hands
are folded in front of her,
like we are in church.

Matt, you've been through so much,
she says, *but we want you*
to stop running,
or, at least, to find out
what it is you're running from.

What is she talking about?
I'm *not* running.
I'm trying to stay.

≡

Dad takes a deep breath.
Let's start at the beginning.
You know that Jeff
was a medic in Vietnam.

I nod but don't look
at anyone.
I try to think about
the circles in the wood,
and whether they'll let me
take my sneakers
and my glove.
I'd like to take my glove.

Dad's voice
keeps breaking through.
They're not always pleasant
to look at.
Some of them have missing fingers
and arms
or even legs.

Who is he talking about?
How does he know?

Even the ones who look fine
have scars.

Scars on the inside, Jeff says.
I've never heard Jeff talk so much.

Maybe you can help them, Matt.
It might mean something
to see they made a difference.

And maybe, Matt,
my mother says softly,
maybe it will help you too.

So they are not
sending me away?

≡

Veteran Voices, or VV,
meets every other Thursday night
at the Community Center.
The Community Center
is an old school
that got converted
into town offices.
My mother takes me there
to see the room ahead of time
so I know what to expect.

It's just the two of us
in the car. Her hands
grip the steering wheel.
If you don't want to do this,
just tell us, Matt, she says.

I feel like I'm riding
in an elevator
that won't stop climbing.
My heart is rising, pumping
in my head, but my stomach
is dropping down.
I'm okay, I say.

To get to the VV room,
we have to walk through
a long, dark hall
beyond a staircase.
There's a small
storage room
behind the
janitor's closet.
Its shelves are packed with
half-empty cartons
of cleaning supplies
and unopened boxes
of tissues.

I try to imagine it
filled with Vietnam veterans,
but all I can picture
are paper lanterns
and fairy-tale dragons.

≡

I still have the elevator
feeling on meeting night.
This time Dad is with me.
It's strange to see him
in his navy jacket
with the big gold buttons,
and his clean white shirt
and gray pants.
He takes off his tie, but
he's still all over too shiny.

I couldn't imagine
what they'd look like,
but I didn't picture them like this.
I didn't picture them
in worn leather vests
or denim jackets with
a rainbow peace sign
sewn on the back,
in dirty sneakered feet,
and muddy army boots
that look like they just
stepped out of a jungle.

They don't look like soldiers.
They just look like
beat-up men.

≡

Jeff is already here.
His face is unshaved,
and he has on a wrinkled
T-shirt instead of his usual
neat white shirt with
the lizard on it.

Even so, Jeff is
different from
everyone else here.
I can't imagine him
crouched in a trench.
I can't imagine
his made-for-music hands
holding a weapon
or wiping blood from
someone's torn-up face.

≡

It looks like there's been a meeting,
but it's already over.
People are standing or sitting,
holding cardboard cups
with pull-out handles
and talking quietly.

Jeff is sitting down at a small table,
talking to a guy in a wheelchair,
but he stands up and heads toward us
when we walk in.

Hi, Matt, Michael.
Dad nods.
I want you to meet someone, Jeff says.
He puts his hand on my shoulder
and gently guides me
toward the table
where he had been talking.
I'll be right there, Dad says. *There's someone
I need to say hello to first.*

The room suddenly feels stuffy,
and the smell of old books
and burnt coffee
makes me nauseous.

Usually I like those smells,
but now I feel sick.
The room has gotten quieter.
I need fresh air,
but Jeff doesn't seem to notice.

Matt, this is Christopher.
I take my hand out of my pocket
to shake Christopher's hand,
but he doesn't move
so I pull it back.

Scars run in every direction
on Christopher's face,
but his eyes are a clear, light blue,
like small circles of pool water
spilled on the craters of the moon.

Christopher's a baseball fan.
Used to play too—we called him Whirlin' Will.
He was a pitcher like you—

Until the war came.

Jeff doesn't say it,
but I know it's true.

I feel Dad's hand
on my shoulder.
Hi, Chris, he says.
He reaches out
to shake Christopher's hand
and when Christopher
doesn't offer one,
Dad just grabs the stump
that's there instead.

I hadn't seen it before.
Why didn't Jeff warn me?

Dad and Christopher
look at each other a long time
without saying anything.
Finally Dad smiles.
Christopher doesn't.
Even if he wanted to,
he couldn't.
His scars move
in the wrong direction.

How's Elizabeth? Christopher asks.
Dad still hasn't looked away.

She's doing well, real well.
You know, Chris, he starts to say,
but stops, leaving his thought
hovering in the air.
I was sorry to hear about Celia,
he says instead,
and his unfinished sentence
floats away.

Yeah, well, it's not your fault,
Christopher finally mumbles,
and when he speaks,
the lines on his face
move like cracks of dried mud.

Dad never mentioned
Christopher before,
but he must have gone
to high school with him
because he starts telling stories
about all the high school
friends he *does* talk about.
Christopher doesn't say anything,
so Dad just keeps on talking
like he does with me,
talking just to fill the silence.

Eventually Dad pauses, like he's
run out of things to say.
He takes a deep breath.
Matt reminds me of you, Chris,
he says. *Sometimes the batter*
doesn't even know
the ball's been pitched!

Yeah, that's what
Jeff says,
Christopher answers.
He takes his eyes
off Dad and
for the first time
looks at me.

My nausea
is gone,
but my stomach
feels empty
and floaty.

I want to smile,
but my face is stuck.

≡

On the way home,
Dad is quiet.
A dark quiet.

How come Jeff called Christopher
Whirlin' Will when his name is Chris?
I ask, trying to fill the silence.

His last name is Williams,
Chris Williams,
Dad says, and then leaves me
for his own thoughts again.

Who's Celia? I ask.

Chris's wife, he says without
turning his head to look at me.

Did she die?

No, she left.

We ride in silence
until Dad shakes his head like
he's waking from a dream.

Chris and Celia were
high school sweethearts.
We all envied their relationship.
But the war changed Chris.

The war changed
all of us, Matt.

Whether we went,
or whether we stayed,
the war changed us all.

≡

When we get back to the house,
we can hear Tommy splashing
upstairs in the tub.
Be right down, my mother calls.
Dad puts his jacket on the banister
and goes to the fridge.
He unwraps some leftover
apple pie, but covers it again
and grabs a beer.
Want anything? he asks.
I shake my head and
he goes right on talking.
Mom, Celia, Chris, and me,
we used to be good friends. . . .
He leaves his sentence
hanging in the air.

Sometimes the words people don't say
are as powerful as the ones they do.

Until the war came,
I say, finishing his thought.

He nods.

Until the war came
and ruined everything.

Because of you, Matt-the-rat,
there's no place for me.

Because of you, my wife left.

Because of you, my brother died.

Because of you, I have stumps instead of legs.

My head starts to spin.

The kitchen suddenly feels
as small as the storage room
behind the janitor's closet.

I'd better go finish my homework, Dad,
I say.
Instead,
I run downstairs
to the basement bathroom
and throw up.

≣

You don't have to go back
if you're not comfortable,
my mother says.

I'm here if you want to talk
about anything,
my father says.

If you give it a chance,
I think it will work out
for everyone,
Jeff says.

I will go back,
but I don't want
to talk about it.

I hope it works
out for someone,
maybe even
for me.

≡

No one asks me any questions,
but I have a question.

Dad, how come you didn't go
to Vietnam?

It's Friday night and we
are clearing the table.
He drops the crusty casserole dish
into the soapy water
and sits back down.

Because I went to medical school.
It was a legitimate deferment.
Ever since I was a kid,
I wanted to be a doctor.

When I was young—
younger than you are now—
I saw a small sparrow
fall out of her nest.
I thought she was hurt.
I went to get a towel to wrap her in
and some bread to feed her,
but when I got back,
she was already gone.

I was happy she'd flown away
but disappointed too.
I wanted to help her.

Be a doctor, Grandpa said.
There'll always be more
than enough wounded people.

Dad taps his hand
on the empty table.

It seemed like
the right thing to do
back then.
But sometimes
I look at Chris and Jeff,
and I wonder,
was it enough?

≡

At night,
through the walls,
I hear them talk.

Stop feeling guilty,
she says.
You did what you thought
was best.
You followed your heart
in a world that had gone
crazy.

I can't help it,
Elizabeth.

That cold fish
shimmies inside me
again.

Maybe for Dad
I'm like the coin
you drop in the poor box
at church.

≡

Saturday is cold.
Too cold
to play baseball,
but we do.

Tommy is at
Mrs. Pennotti's house.
My parents are sitting
on the top bleacher
where they always
sit when Tommy
doesn't come.

The sun is behind
a thick blanket
of clouds.
The warm-ups
don't warm me up.

My arm feels stiff.

I know it's cold out here,
Coach Robeson says,
coughing into his sleeve.
Just play your best.

≡

Woo-hoo, my mother calls

the first two batters.
The umpire shakes his head.
The batters are just too cold
to swing their bats.
The third player up
glares at me.
I take off my glove
and stick it under my arm.
I smudge the ball and get ready
to pitch.

The ball sails right down
the middle of the plate.
Crack.
The crowd cheers.
A home run.

I hear my father's voice.
It's okay, Matt! You'll get the next one.
The next batter gets a base hit,
but I do strike out the following one.

It's early in the game,
Coach Robeson says to me

as we head into the dugout.
You'll warm up.

Hey, Frog-face,
Rob says on his way
to the batter's box.
Playin' for the other team today?
There's no time to react.

Rob hits a single.
So does Alex.
Daniel drives in a run
on a double.

The score stays tied
until the sixth inning.
Then I hit a single.
Rob follows with a double
and I race home.
We squeak by
with a 2–1 victory.

Lucky little Frog-face,
Billy says.

≡

My mother
is making dinner,
so I need to
watch Tommy.

It's drizzling outside.
We can't toss the ball.

Instead I pile
Tommy's alphabet blocks
and he knocks them down.

I make a barn
for his farm animals
and he oinks and moos.

He climbs on my back
and babbles,
Giddy-yap, Matt,
giddy-yap, Matt.

He kicks the sides
of me with his
soft
bare
feet.

≡

Tuesday just before the final bell,
a huge storm cloud
rolls in unexpectedly.
Squat close to the ground
like a heaving monster,
it hurls heavy black
drops of rain
that bounce rather than fall.

Track is canceled,
the end-of-the-day voice
announces.
The baseball team
should meet in the gym.

Make a circle, Coach says,
tossing fourteen
dirty, ripped, partially split
baseballs into the center.
Everybody grab a baseball;
we're going to take a peek inside.

It isn't easy,
but I pull off the leather cover.
Inside is a layer of thin twine.
Beneath that are layers

and layers of wool yarn
specked with small pieces
of red thread.

Start unraveling, Coach Robeson says.
Roll the ball if that makes it easier.

It's hard not to laugh
as the yarn unrolls
and the unwrapped baseballs
zoom in every direction.
I'm careful to keep my baseball
away from Rob,
but he isn't paying attention
to me anyway.
He and some of the other guys
have gotten themselves
all twisted and tangled.

Only my baseball unwinds
in a solitary path
across the gleaming gym floor.

≡

When yards and yards of yarn
are unfurled,
small rubber balls
start bouncing everywhere.

Coach Robeson watches for a while
and then calls for everyone
to settle down in a circle again.

How many of you think
you've reached the heart of the ball? he asks.
All fourteen hands
shoot into the air.

You haven't. Coach Robeson laughs.
If you cut deeper, you'd find
the black rubber piece
is just another protective layer.
Inside that is the heart of the ball,
a small molded core of cork.

Coach Robeson talks about
the baseball's design and
how it helps us to hit farther.

Sometimes it's useful
to open things up
and have a closer look.
Sometimes it helps
to understand why things
work the way they do.

I don't think dissecting
a baseball is going to make
me play better or
understand anything better,
but I put all the broken pieces
in my pocket.

≡

Thursday night,
the elevator feeling
is there again
but fainter this time.

Dad comes home early.

We eat quickly—
no dessert—
so we can arrive on time.

When we get there,
Jeff is standing
in front of the room
talking about oranges.

He is asking everyone
to sign a petition
so the government
will do a study
on vets who ate oranges
and got sick.

Dad whispers in my ear,
Agent Orange is a chemical.

It was used to destroy
forests and crops in Vietnam,
but now
it's making soldiers sick.

I'm glad no one can read my mind.
Agent Orange,
not regular oranges,
a chemical,
not a fruit that soldiers ate.

I wonder if anyone here
ever sprayed Agent Orange on
any of the plants I touched,
any of the places I walked,
any of the people I loved.

≡

When Jeff finishes talking,
all the vets who can
scrape their chairs into a circle.
The ones who can't—
who have withered hands
or clumsy wheelchairs
with wheels that won't turn—
are brought into the circle
by the stronger ones.

No one is left out.

Dad and I push back our chairs,
and Chris uses his good hand
to move his wheelchair next to us.

Then the vets and visitors
go around the circle
spilling stories.
Not everyone talks,
but the ones who do
talk a lot,
like an opened fire hydrant
gushing words and tears
instead of water.

≡

Anybody here figured out a way
to turn it off?
Joe, the guy who is talking,
wears a T-shirt that says
BOX OF RAIN.
He has a red bandanna
wrapped around his forehead, and
his hair is wild and bushy.
He looks like a caveman in a T-shirt.
He looks like he should have a deep,
booming voice, but instead
he sounds hollow,
like a wounded lamb.

I see their faces everywhere, he says,
I hear their screamin' and their cryin',
Help me. I don't want to die.
His voice gets quiet.
I wiped the blood and grime off his face.
I told him he wasn't gonna die,
to just hang on 'cause he wasn't
gonna die. I told him the Dustoff'd
be comin' soon, even though I knew
no Dustoff was gonna find us
in that mud hole.
He was gonna die

right there in my arms.
I knew it, and he knew it,
but we kept holdin' on,
pretendin' we could hold on forever.
He knew he was dying, we both knew.
He was already gone when
I took him in my arms,
but we both kept holdin' on.
Pretendin'. I'm still pretendin'.
For the rest of my life, I'll be pretendin'.
How ya doing? they ask,
and I say,
Okay, man,
even though I'm not.
I'm not okay,
and I'm never gonna be okay again.
I just don't get it, how they don't see my
insides hangin' out, when it's all I can do
to put these feelings into words
because words don't mean
a thing.

There was a silent pause,
a *pausa di breve,*
like a caesura,
the railroad mark

on the top line of the staff,
telling us to stop,
to wait,
not to rush through.

Music is soothing.

Music is not like words.

Words are messy.
Words spill out
like splattered blood,
oozing in every direction,
leaving stains
that won't come out
no matter how hard you scrub.

But not music.
Even when it's so loud
you can't hear anything else,
music lulls you to sleep.

Right now,
I need music.

≡

Someone else starts talking,
pulling me out of my mind,
pulling me back to the room
beyond the staircase,
behind the janitor's closet,
where words are spilling
and splattering in every direction.

If I close my eyes,
I can still smell the stench,
this vet says.
I can still see the children
running toward us,
explosives strapped on their
backs, running toward us,
and then dropping like
scarecrows.
I can still hear them scream.

His shoulders heave.
Jeff puts his arm around him
but doesn't say anything.
Nobody says anything,
but the silence is like
a warm blanket
we wrap around him.

≡

That night,
it's hard to sleep.
I wonder what Jeff
and Joe
and Chris would say
if they knew
my story,

if I broke open
the circle
and told them.

What would Dad say?
And my mother?
Would she still ask
me to watch Tommy
while she made dinner?

Or would she
pick him up
and push me away?

≡

Coach Robeson isn't at practice
on Monday.
Coach Louis starts us off
with a jog around the field.
Is Coach Robeson coming?
Drew asks.
Everyone laughs.
Drew hates to run.
If Coach Robeson isn't coming,
he'll slow his pace.
Maybe we'll run some extra laps
before we practice our batting,
Coach Louis says
and doesn't even smile.

≡

Coach Robeson isn't at practice
Tuesday or Wednesday.
When he comes to the field
Thursday, he looks different,
thinner and tired.
He waves us over, and we sit
on the bleachers.

Sorry I haven't been here, boys.
You know I'd never miss a practice
if I could help it.
He takes a deep breath and coughs
into a big white handkerchief.

I'm afraid I need to take
a break for a while—
Nobody says anything and
Coach takes another deep breath.
He looks at us a long moment,
his tired eyes taking each of us in
and holding us.
I've had this cough that just wouldn't
go away—so I finally had it checked.

He clears his throat.
Turns out I need to have an operation
and then some treatments.
The treatments might
make me sick, so I've gotta
give up coaching for a while.
Don't worry, I'm looking into
getting someone else
to take my place.
Someone you'll really learn from.
I hope I'll be back.
I can't promise you,
but I'm hoping.
Coach coughs
into his handkerchief again
and blots both his eyes.
Continue to play your best because
whether I'm on the field or not,
I'll be rooting for you.

Before he leaves,
he looks at me and nods.

I hope it's not good-bye.

≡

At the dinner table,
I ask Dad how a person
can be so sick
and not look sick at all.

Some cancers are sneaky.
They're silent and invisible.
They creep up on you
and invade so deep on the inside
that no one on the outside
even knows the cancer's there
until it's too late.

My mother stirs the soup
and ladles it into my bowl.
Some cancers can be cured
if they're caught early, she says,

as if cancer were a tossed ball
and if you catch it on a fly,
there's no chance of death
scoring a run.
Maybe Coach can still
beat it, but it sounds
like the bases

are loaded against him.

What can we do?

*All we can do is show him
how much we care,* she says.

*How about throwing him a dinner
at the Pavilion?* I ask.

My mother pauses,
then smiles.

*I'll call Mrs. Brennan.
We'll see what we can do.*

≡

Fire in the darkness
blood
pounding rain
and smoke.
The smell of burning.

I'm sinking in mud.
Help! Someone help me,
please!

Eyes are watching.
Waiting.
I can't follow,
something binds my legs.

My arms are heavy,
someone groans—

Matt, Matt, wake up.
You're having a nightmare.

I sit up in bed,
sweaty and scared.
He brings me a glass of cold water.

138   She touches my face.
        Her hands are soft and cool.
        I close my eyes
        and lie back down.

        I listen.

        We have found you and we love you.
        You will never be alone.

        I will sing to you of morning,
        I will stay until it's light.
        I will sing to you of laughter
        on the other side of night.

        ≡

Across the street
from Rosie O's Pizza Planet
is the Pavilion.

The Pavilion is a big,
blue marble building.
Different size rooms
surround a huge indoor fountain.
All the sports dinners
and school graduations,
all the parties and proms
are at the Pavilion.
A lot of business people
go there too.
It's the fanciest place
in town.
Unless we want to wait,
there's only one
small room available
for Coach Robeson.

We don't want to wait.

On Friday night, we invite him
to the Pavilion's Green Room.

At dinner while we
eat our salad,
Rob's father, Mr. Brennan,
stands at a podium
in the front of the room.
The podium is set up
at the top of three
wide red-carpeted stairs
so everyone can see.

Rob's father is telling us
how great Coach Robeson is,
what a wonderful role model,
how much we'll all miss him.
*The program won't be the same
without him,* he says.

I pick at the pale lettuce
and red onion circles.
I stack the green peppers
in the middle
like a vegetable volcano.

Why is he talking like
Coach Robeson is
already dead?

≡

Mr. Brennan says
we shouldn't wait
to thank people
for the good they do.
He doesn't want
another moment to go by
without thanking Coach Robeson
for all the good
he's done.

He looks at Coach
and starts to tell a story
about Rob's brother, but his voice
begins to quaver.
He just stands there
trying to talk and stopping
until Coach gets up
and climbs the stairs to the podium.
Mr. Brennan and Coach Robeson
look at each other a minute,
shake hands, and then
pull each other into a hug.

Mr. Brennan leaves the podium,
and Mrs. Brennan squeezes
through the tables to meet him.

They lean into each other and
Mrs. Brennan buries her head
in Mr. Brennan's shoulder.
They walk back to their table
like some lost
two-headed creature.

I look over at Rob.
He's slouched in his chair,
wiping his eyes
with the sleeve of his shirt.
He glares at me
when he sees me look at him
and straightens up again
when his parents sit down.

≡

Coach Robeson
thanks everyone
for their kind words,
their thoughts,
and their prayers.

Behind the podium
Coach looks smaller
than he ever did
in the gym
or on the field.
It's like he's already
disappearing.
I play with
my Russian lava dressing,
hiding the onions
underneath the lettuce,
trying to keep the lava
from oozing out.

Dad taps me on the shoulder
to listen.

Facing cancer
is the toughest thing
I've ever done, Coach says.

But it's not half as tough
as what some of you have faced.
Not half as tough
as sending your kids off to war.
The real role models
are Ray and Chris,
Sam and AJ,
kids who graduated
from high school
and put off going to college
to fight in a war,
especially a war
that's been so divisive.
Kids who gave up their youth—
and for some, their lives.

Then Coach quickly
changes the subject
and starts talking
about cancer.
Most of the time grown-ups
talk to other grown-ups,
but I can tell that Coach
is talking to us,
to the kids on his team.
I'll lick this disease if I can,

he says,
but I can't promise you I will.
Still, you've gotta play your best
even if you're losing.
You've always gotta give it
your best shot.

His eyes lock into mine.
I want to jump up and
promise him I will, but
I'm stuck to my chair.
There's no fire or
sinking mud, but
something binds my legs—
just like in my nightmare.

Why can't I ever say the things
I want to say?

I smash my salad volcano
so that lava dressing runs in
every direction on the plate.

Coach says he'll still try
to come to our games
whenever he can.

You'll do well, if you
continue to work together,
he says.
That's what sports is all about,
learning to work together.

I hear Coach talk,
but I'm stuck in Vietnam
with the smell and the smoke
and the sound of someone crying.

Maybe the Americans
should have brought baseballs
instead of bombs.

≡

Until they find a full-time
replacement for Coach Robeson,
Mr. Chambers, a math teacher
and the girls' basketball coach,
is helping Coach Louis.

His practices don't run as long
because off-season
he's also the moderator
of the debating club,
and they're getting ready
for a state tournament.

Without Coach Robeson,
Rob is free to
accidentally
step on my jacket,
or dump my books.

So sorry, Frog-face,
I must have lost
my focus.

148   Shorter practices
leave me more time
to practice my scales.
My fingers climb up
the keys perfectly now.
I only stumble
sometimes on the
way back down
when I get close
to middle C.

≡

While I run
my fingers
up and down
the keys,
Tommy drives his
yellow bus underneath
the piano bench.
Let's let Matt
practice in peace,
my mother says.
She picks up Tommy
and smiles at me.
Sounds good, she says.

Sounds good,
Jeff agrees on Wednesday.
You've got a nice touch, Matt.
Not too heavy, not too soft,

just right.

≡

On Thursday night,
before Dad gets home,
I finish all my homework.
I practice the piano,
I take out the garbage,
I even clean out
Tommy's toy box.

The elevator
feeling
is gone.

I can't wait
to walk with Dad
down the hall,
behind the janitor's closet,
to the small, crowded
room behind the stairs.

I *want*
to go.

I *want*
to remember.

She held me
and sang a soft song.

He followed me
everywhere,

he follows me still.

The business part of the meeting
lasts only a few minutes
and before long
we are scraping ourselves
into a circle.

Jeff's hand is on my shoulder.

*Are you sure
it's okay?* he asks.
I nod.

I know there will be no daring
dragon prince who fled
behind the mountain.
I wonder what Jeff will say
instead.

He pulls a piece of paper
out of his pocket, unfolds it,
and starts to talk.

*Hope you don't mind,
but I wrote my thoughts down
so I wouldn't forget anything.*

My stomach does a quick flip.
Jeff begins to speak quietly.

≡

For the past few meetings,
I've brought my friend Matt
with me, he says, nodding
at me and smiling.

A lot of you have asked
who he is and why he's here.
Some of you find it upsetting
to have a Vietnamese kid
sitting here, reminding you
of the place
we all want to forget.
Others want to know
what he knows.

Hearing Jeff talk about me
is a little like floating underwater;
I can hear him,
his voice is clear,
but distant too.
Even though I went to all those
Saturday classes
at the adoption agency,
it's strange
to be called
a Vietnamese kid.

154   What does that mean?
I know it doesn't mean
believing in mountain fairies
or celebrating Tet Trung Thu.
I know it means
something else,

but I'm not sure what.

☰

Matt was one of the older kids
airlifted out of Saigon,
Jeff says.

He's reading a sentence at a time
and then looking up.

He was almost ten, but he looked six.

He was born during the war.

His whole life was the war.

He's got an American father
who left and never came back.

He's got a mother who
entrusted him to us
even though his father,
an American soldier,
ran out on her.

She gave her child to a bunch
of American soldiers . . .

Jeff emphasizes the first syllable
in soldiers
as if it were *soul*diers,

. . . so we must have done
something good.

Americans who've never
been to Vietnam
don't understand.
They spit at us.
They call us baby killers.
But we can't have been all bad,
or what mother
would have given us her child,
knowing she might never
see him again?

What kind of faith is that?
What kind of love?

Love?

I thought she wanted
me to leave because of

who I was and what
I'd done.

But did she mean it
when she said she loved me?
Did he mean it
when he said he loved her?
Was it hard for her to
push me away?
Does she ever wonder
about me
like I wonder
about her
and about him?

Does she remember me?

Jeff's words rush through me,
my heart pounds, and
a red hotness spreads
across my face.

I hadn't ever thought
she gave me away
because she loved me.

≡

We lost a big piece
of ourselves in Vietnam,
and none of us will
ever be the same,
but we did some good too.
We made a difference.
Don't let anybody tell you
different.

Jeff looks at everyone in the circle
one by one,
holding their eyes with his eyes
before turning away.

Next time someone stares at you
like you're a freak
because you went to Vietnam,
think about Matt,
and there are hundreds like him,
hundreds of kids we saved.

Jeff finishes talking, and
he seems quiet again,
like the Jeff who lets

his music speak for him.
He asks if I have anything
I want to say, and Dad gives me
an encouraging nod,
but I shake my head.

≡

Jeff's words change the mood.
The next two people talk
about Vietnamese friends,
the boy with his face burned off
who learned
to sing "Yankee Doodle,"
the old man who sat outside
one vet's hooch waiting
to offer homemade rice wine
to thank him for taking
such good care
of his sick daughter.

Slowly the heaviness
in the room lifts,
the stories stop coming,
and the circle is broken.

Dad is tossing away
Chris's Coke can
when another man
in a wheelchair
rolls over to me.

Thanks for coming,
he says.
Don't think too badly
of your birth father.
It's hard to come home,
but it's harder to go back.

It doesn't mean he didn't care.

≡

In the car
we are quiet for a while
and then Dad asks me if
I have any thoughts about
what Jeff said.

I shake my head.

Do you ever think about Vietnam?
he asks, taking his eyes
off the road
and looking at me.

I shrug.

It's okay
if you don't want
to talk about it right now,
he says.
But someday,
I hope you will.

That night when I go
to sleep, I hear her voice
whispering,
Bui Doi,
you cannot stay here.

I try to follow her.

I want to follow,

but I fall asleep,
and I don't wake up
until morning.

On Wednesday afternoon,
Coach Chambers tells us
there will be a new coach
starting the following Monday.
He doesn't tell us anything
about him except to say
he has a lot of experience
and we should treat him
with respect.

He glances at Coach Louis
and adds, *Handpicked*
by Coach Robeson,
so you know he's good.

He'd better be
better than good.
We're more than halfway
through the season
and our record is 7–2.
We have a shot
at the championship.

We've got two games
over the weekend.
On Saturday, I'm surprised to see

Chris's wheelchair parked next to
the bottom bleacher.
Jeff and my parents
are sitting beside him.
I am even more surprised
on Sunday
when Chris is scribbling
on Coach's clipboard.

By Monday,
I'm not surprised at all,
but the other kids are.

≡

Chris wheels himself
onto the field.
Before we start our stretches,
Coach Chambers introduces him
as Coach Williams.
He nods and tries to smile.
In the sunlight
his scars run deeper,
stained with different shades
of red, purple, and blue.
I've watched you play, boys.
You're good.
But Coach Robeson and I
have some ideas
to help you get better.

Yeah, well, Billy says, *we'll just wait*
for Coach Robeson to come back.

Then everyone starts talking
at once.

What is Robeson thinking?
How can he coach us when he can't even walk?
We might as well give up our trophy now.
Maybe the cancer has spread to his brain.

What *was* Coach Robeson thinking?
If I had scars like that,
I'd never go outside again.
But Chris didn't do anything
to those kids.
How can they be so mean?
Leave him alone, I say.
Give him a chance!

Shut up, Frog-face, Rob answers.
He knocks me down.
Suddenly his knee
is on top of my chest,
his fist is in my face,
and Billy is standing
above me.

Finally the whistle blows
so long and loud
it hurts my ears.
Coach Louis pulls Rob off me.
That's enough of that.
Coach Williams's voice
is stern but calm.
Begin your stretches, he says.

≡

On Tuesday afternoon,
Coach Robeson is back
to tell us
what he's thinking.

He walks onto the field
slowly.
He looks thinner
but still not sick.

For a minute, I think
his leaving
is just another nightmare,
and now that it's daylight,
he's going to partner us up
and tell us to start stretching.

Instead
he motions for us
to sit down.
He takes a breath.

His voice sounds like
he's whistling through a straw,
only instead of blowing air,

he's blowing words,
thin, wavy, watery words
that mean something
even though he barely
has the power
to say them.

☰

Coach Williams was a student of mine,
he manages.
His eyes move first to Rob,
then to me,
then to each player
one at a time.

When I first met him,
he was the same age as you.
We called him Whirlin' Will.
The way that baseball danced,
no one could get a hit off him.
I followed his career into high school.
I follow all my boys,
but I knew that Chris
had what it took.
Baseball was more than a game
to Chris.
If anyone was going
to play in college, maybe even
get scouted for the majors,
it was going to be Chris Williams.
Coach takes another breath,
swallows, and continues.

But, it didn't happen that way, did it?
The war changed a lot of things
and a lot of people. I'm not going to argue
for or against; that's not my place.
But I can tell you, the war was worse
than this cancer I got.
It destroyed us
from the inside.
While we were going about our business,
while we were working, or studying,
or playing baseball,
the war was working against us,
spreading its poison.

Coach coughs into his fist.
He waits a moment,
then continues.

It's still spreading its poison,
and I don't know
of any treatment that can stop it.
That's up to you.

Chris Williams isn't going
to make it to the major league.

But that doesn't mean he can't be useful.
That doesn't mean he can't be a part
of the game he loves.
And he doesn't need to park his wheelchair
and simply watch.
Baseball isn't only athletics.
You should know that by now.
You don't just pitch or swing with your arm.
Baseball's about concentration.
Focus.
Coach Robeson looks right at me.
Then he looks at Rob.
There's no reason Coach Williams
can't coach, except maybe
you won't let him.

Coach Robeson swallows again.
Just talking seems to tire him out.

People see that withered arm,
those wheels and scars,
and they think they know
everything about him.
What can they learn
from someone so beat-up?

But I'll tell you something,
even if I hadn't gotten sick,
I was going to ask Chris
to be my pitching coach.

Coach takes another deep breath.
His eyes are drained of color,
tired and gray.

You're a good group of kids,
but you've got some mixed-up attitudes,
which you probably learned from us adults.
Now officially I'm not your coach anymore.
So maybe some of you think
you don't have to listen to me,
but I hope you will.
I've always told you the truth.

Give Coach Williams a chance.
Give each other a chance.

I look over at Rob.
His arms are crossed
in front of him.
He doesn't seem to be listening
to Coach Robeson at all.
He won't even look
in his direction.
His eyes are angry bullets
aimed somewhere
beyond him.

Coach Robeson looks
deflated—like the
wrinkled remains
of a balloon
that's had all the air
let out.

He nods at Coach Chambers
and then turns to walk
across the field

and away from us.

From the back,
Coach Robeson looks

sad and solitary.
I won't let anyone know—
especially Rob—
but a ball of tears
is stuck in my throat.

≡

My mother is waiting
for me in the car.
Are you okay?

I nod.

She watches me,
disbelieving,
her clear eyes
a flashing bolt of light
that sees straight
through me.
Was that Coach Robeson?
Did he come to today's practice?

I nod again.

How did he seem?

Okay.
Where's Tommy? I ask.

I left him with Mrs. P.
Dad's going to be late,
so I thought we could

grab a hamburger.
Just the two of us.

I look at her.
Her open, kind face.
Her encouraging smile.
She tries so hard.
All the time
she tries so hard.
Sometimes,
when I'm doing my homework,
she brings me cookies,
or an orange, already peeled,
broken into small pieces.
Here, take a break, have a snack,
she says.

A hamburger sounds good,
I say.
I'm hungry.

≡

On Wednesday,
Coach Williams
is waiting for us
on the field.

Baseballs, mitts,
masks, helmets,
all sorts of sports stuff
are scattered on the ground.
It looks like somebody
robbed the athletic office,
then panicked,
and dropped everything
as they ran off
across the field.

*What happened here,
a tornado?* Billy says.

I'm not cleaning it up, Rob says.

Ignoring the mess
and the comments,
Coach Williams
partners us up.

My name is called first,
then Rob's.
After what happened
on his first day,
something must be wrong with
Coach Williams's brain.

≡

Rob glares at me
and mouths the words
No way, Frog-face,
but Coach Williams
is already wheeling around,
using some kind of
cane with claws
to shift the equipment,
a little to the left,
a little to the right,
like there's a pattern.
If there is,
I don't see it.

We wait for some direction.

We're going to try
something new.
Coach Williams's voice is husky,
but his words are clear.
He calls one kid
from each pair
to get a bandanna
from a bag
he has clipped
to his chair.

Rob gets called for us.
When everyone is
back with his partner,
Coach Williams
instructs each person
holding a bandanna to tie it tight
around his eyes.

I don't want you to see any light,
he says.

Rob mumbles something
I can't hear.
Everyone else is laughing.
Hey, that's not tight enough . . .
double it up . . . you're cheating . . .
how many fingers am I holding up? . . .
wrong . . .

Enough!
Coach Williams says sternly.
Everyone shuts up.

On the ground, there are
seven baseballs, seven footballs,

and seven soccer balls, he says.
Seven helmets, seven catcher's masks,
seven bats, and seven mitts.
We have seven teams of two.
When I say Go,
those of you wearing bandannas
need to gather one of each—
one baseball, one football, one bat—
you know what I mean.

Those of us without bandannas
look around.

If you paid close attention,
you might remember
where you saw things,
but after a while
it isn't going to matter
what you remember.
After you've turned around
a couple of times in the dark,
you'll get disoriented.
Eventually your partner
will need to be your eyes.
When you pick up all seven items,

work your way back to the bleachers,
sit down, and wait
for the rest of your teammates.
Any questions?

There's some grumbling
and one *What does this have to do*
with baseball?
spoken under Rob's breath,
but if Coach hears,
he doesn't answer.

≡

When Coach says *Go,*
Rob starts walking
ahead of me
using his right foot
to guide him.
I try to look like
I'm doing something,
but really I'm just
following behind.
Rob picks up a football,
a bat, and a mitt.
When it's too awkward
to hold them and still search,
he reaches for me.
Without a word,
he holds out his hand,
feels my presence,
and drops the football
and the mitt into my arms.
He uses the bat
to feel around the ground.
Whatever Coach Williams's
reason is for this game,

Rob has made up
his own challenge—

getting through it
without saying
one word
to me.

He might have done it too—
the baseball and helmet
are just inches from each other,
and two soccer balls have rolled
alongside them.

The only kids who aren't
at the bleachers already
are me and Rob,
and Michael V. and Alex.

We can hear Alex telling Michael
where to walk for the soccer ball.
Rob follows his voice.
I follow Rob.

Our last item
is the catcher's mask.
Alex must feel sorry for Rob,
or for me.
The catcher's mask
is way out in right field,
he calls as he and Michael
make their way
back to the bleachers.

Still, knowing where the mask is
won't help much
if I can't get Rob moving
in the right direction.

Everyone on the bleachers
is laughing and heckling us.

If I don't help Rob,
we'll be walking
in circles till midnight.

We're moving
in the wrong direction.

I clear my throat.
Rob, I whisper loudly.
Just let me lead you.
If you don't let me help,
we'll be out here all afternoon.

I'm never
gonna need your help
for anything,
Frog-face.

I can't see Rob's eyes,
but I think they might
burn holes
right through
his bandanna.

I hate you,
he says.
*My brother died
because of you.*

≡

His words hit me
like a fastball
in the pit of my stomach.

I think I might crumble
right there on the field
with Rob stumbling along
in his own private darkness
and the voices of
Coach Robeson and Dad
talking about war and cancer
stuck in my head—
The war was worse
than this cancer I've got.
Some cancers are sneaky,
they creep up on you.
Over and over
I hear Caveman Joe spending
the rest of his life pretendin'
and Jeff calling me a Vietnamese kid,
the one who reminds everyone
of the place they all want to forget.
I hear the laughter in the bleachers
and the sound of her voice shrieking
Bui Doi, you cannot stay here
while helicopters whirl
and babies cry.

In the distance,
bombs fall,
dogs bark,

and then I hear her voice,
like warm honey, softly singing.

There is darkness on the water.
There is darkness on the land.
There is darkness all around us,
but I will take your hand.

I will sing to you of morning,
I will stay until it's light.
I will sing to you of laughter
on the other side of night.

I take a big gulp of air,
a big gulp of sunlight.

You've gotta play your best even if you're losing.
You'll always be our MVP.
What kind of faith is that? What kind of love?

I force myself to breathe.

I want to find that place.

≡

I lost my brother too,
I say, and
my words
surprise me.
He isn't dead,
but he's gone just the same.
And it's my fault.
My mouth is saying stuff
I don't even know I'm thinking.
I'm sorry that your brother died.
I'm really sorry.
I know how you feel.

You don't know anything,
Rob says, but his voice
is more sad than angry.
He still has his bandanna on,
and I can't see his eyes,
but I don't think they're
bullets anymore.

Every Friday night,
he'd take me to Rosie O's,
he says.
His voice is quiet,
like he's talking to himself
and letting me listen.

Just the two of us.
Sometimes we went to the movies
or to the sports department at Sears.
He came to all my games too.
When he came back,
we were going to get
Yankee tickets.
That was the last thing
he said to me:
When I get back,
we'll get season tickets.

I'm sorry
is all I can think
to say.

≡

My brother was younger
than me, six years
younger than me.

We walk toward the outfield.
Rob follows my voice.

There are so many things
I don't remember, but
I remember that my mother—
my mother in Vietnam—
left us to check on
this old man and woman
who lived down the road.

Sometimes she helped them
with their laundry
or we brought them cooked rice
and vegetables.

I keep talking,
like a bicycle tire
with a slow leak.

The lady's face was burned—
her whole face was burned black

so that her eyes were just slits.
And the fingers of her hand
were fused together.
Her husband was sick too,
so people in the village
took turns helping them.

Every night we'd hear
popping sounds and dogs barking
in the distance,
but we'd just go on eating
and not even look up.

Sometimes the old man and
woman ate with us.
One night, the popping
grew close.

A low hissing sound
came from the sky over us.

Down the road
red and orange flames
chased giant clouds of black smoke.

I thought I'd forgotten everything,
but I hadn't.
I remembered.
I remembered everything.

The next day, my mother
went to check on the old man and his wife.

Watch your brother, she said.
Stay inside, it isn't safe.

But I didn't want to stay inside.
Sometimes the soldiers dropped stuff.

Once I found a metal cross,
another time a silver coin.

I told my brother to wait inside.
I told him I'd be right back.

But he followed me.
He followed me everywhere.

Just be careful, I said.
But three-year-olds
don't know how to be careful.

It was quiet outside.
Everything smelled of
spoiled eggs and smoke.
The heat was pressing down.
It was hard to breathe.

I knew it would start to rain soon.
I wanted to look for things
before the water
washed everything away.

He wandered away from me,
and before I knew
what was happening,
he was screaming.
There was blood
everywhere.

The rain started slamming down.
I lifted him up
and carried him home.
He was so heavy
that it took a long time.
When I got there,
she was waiting.

She made a long wailing sound
when she saw us.
All those years,
I heard bombs and guns
and people screaming,

but I never heard
a sound like that.

I never heard a sound
like the sound
she made that day.

Finally she got the bleeding to stop,
and we saw that both his legs were gone.
They just weren't there anymore.

The fingers on his hands
were missing too.
His hands were small
mangled stumps.

And even though
she told me it wasn't,

I knew it was all my fault.

☰

When I stop talking,
we stop walking.
The catcher's mask
is at our feet,
but I don't say anything,
and Rob doesn't feel for it.

We both just stand there.

It's strange—
in my dreams,
I can never
see her face,
but when I tell Rob,
I see it all—
like a movie—
I see her face,
open and clear,
her dark eyes
holding me.

I hear her voice,
like on a tape recorder.

It's not your fault.

≡

The mask is by your left foot,
I finally manage.
You'd better pick it up.

Rob pulls off
the bandanna
and looks at me.
His eyes are red.
Are you okay? he asks.

I nod.
He gives me
the bandanna
to wipe my face.

When we finally make it
to the bleachers,
everyone starts cheering.

But not Coach Williams.

He looks at Rob
and then at me.

I hope you and Matt
      can figure out for yourselves
      the purpose of this hunt,
      he says
      and wheels away.

      ☰

Dad picks me up
from practice.
Are you okay? he says.
You look tired.

I'm okay.
It was a long day.

He fiddles with the radio
but doesn't sing.
Every time
he changes the station,
he sneaks a glance at me.

I remember when Jeff
introduced me
at the VV meeting.

Afterward Dad asked me
if I ever thought
about Vietnam.

It's okay
if you don't want
to talk about it right now,
he said.

But someday,
I hope you will.

I need to tell them.
But will I find
the words again?
And what will happen
once I say them?

≡

When we get home,
Tommy and my mother
are outside.
She is raking out
the dead leaves
from the garden.
He is walking
his wooden turtle.
He waddles over
when he sees me.
I put down my books and
pick him up.

Suddenly
I feel like crying again.
It's that fastball,
let loose,
an unexpected
wild pitch,
rolling in my stomach.

≡

After dinner, I help Dad
clear the dishes
while my mother
gives Tommy his bath.
When she comes down again,
instead of watching TV,
I ask them
if we can talk.

We sit at the kitchen table
with its ragged lines like
jagged sideways mountains.

I step back into the jungle
and let the words lead me
where I don't want to go.

≡

I tell them everything
and before they can respond,
I say, *I understand*
if you hate me and
want to send me away.

Hate you? Send you away?
My mother
moves closer to me.
She touches my face
with her soft hands.
Matt, you're our son.
We love you.
Nothing, nothing
will ever change that.

What happened to your brother
wasn't your fault,
Dad says.
The war wasn't your fault.
War is a monster
with a mind of its own.

My brother—
My mother—

I start to say,
my other brother—
my other mother—
The words
choke in my throat.
I breathe deep
and force them out.
Do you think we can
ever try to find them?

And with the words,
hot tears flood my face.

My mother pulls me so close
I can hear her heart.
We will try,
she whispers.

≡

That night
she comes
into my room
and sits at the end
of my bed.
I've just turned off
the light.

Are you sleeping?
she asks.

Not yet.

She leaves the light off,
but the moon shines
through the window,
so I can see her soft,
open face.

I'm glad we talked,
Matt, she says.
I love you so, so much,
and of course,
loving you
doesn't mean

I love Tommy
any less.

She pats my leg.

You can love us both,
Matt. It won't mean
you've forgotten her
or that you didn't care.
The heart always
has room
for more love.
It won't mean
that you've forgotten.

≡

When I see Rob
in the hall
the next day,
I almost look away,
out of habit,
but I don't.
We nod at each other
and keep walking.
In the lunchroom, he asks
if I'm going to practice.
I haven't missed one practice
since the season started.
Neither has he.

Yep,
I answer.
Are you?

≡

We win our division
and will be heading for
the league championship.
The day we win the
final division game,
Coach Robeson
is in the hospital
recuperating
from his operation.
The whole team goes
to Victory Memorial
to visit him.

We have to take turns
going to his room,
two visitors at a time.
Rob and I go upstairs.
Coach's whole face smiles
when he sees us
together.

≡

I hear you two have been
doing great things, he whispers.
I'm proud of you.

Rob and I look at each other.
I nod.
Rob reaches into his jacket pocket
and gives Coach a baseball.

The whole team signed it, he says.

Coach's face isn't so pale anymore,
and his eyes are back
to their old shade of blue.

Thanks, Coach—for everything,
I say.

Mr. Brennan was right.
You shouldn't wait
to thank people
for the good they do.

Words are messy,
but sometimes,
words are all you've got
to show what matters most.

≡

I can't believe how easy
the scales are getting.
Sometimes my fingers
just fly over the keys,
and Jeff has to tell me
to slow down,
to pace myself.

You're good, he says,
but music is not simply
playing notes.
You have to play
the silence too.

≡

I've been thinking
of saying something
at the next VV meeting,
nothing important,
nothing about
my mother in Vietnam
or what happened to
my brother,
but something,
something that would
show them I was there,
that I remember.

Vietnam is beautiful,
I say and
I am not remembering
stories someone told me
or pictures from books.

I am just remembering.

White cabbages grew
as big as pumpkins.
And before a storm,
the purple-blue of the

sky was the same
purple-blue as my
mom's favorite shawl.

My father squeezes
my shoulder.

Caveman Joe nods
like he remembers too.
A couple of the vets
smile.

☰

On Sunday, it rains.
Alex calls and asks
if I would like to go
bowling with the team.

All of my balls end up
in the gutter.
*It's okay to get strikes
in bowling,* Rob says,
and we laugh.
We eat french fries
and drink Coke,
then bowl
some more.

*Maybe you'd better
save your arm
for pitching,*
someone says,
and we all
turn around.

Coach Robeson
stands behind
the blue-and-white

plastic chairs
in our bowling corner.

He's still thin,
but his voice
is stronger,
and he's smiling.

≡

The dinner dishes
are still on the table,
but Mom and Tommy
are already splashing upstairs.
*Sometimes cancer goes
into remission,* Dad explains.
*Sometimes it even
disappears completely
and people get
a second chance.*

We start scraping the dishes
and piling them in the sink.

*Will that happen
with Coach Robeson?*

*I don't know, Matt,
but we can hope.
Everyone deserves
a second chance.*

≡

218

The days are getting
really warm.
Summer is sitting
on spring
and squeezing out
all the wetness.

Tommy and I
spend a lot of time
outside
tossing the ball.
His plastic yellow bat
is bigger than he is,
but he's using it
like a golf club anyway.
He hits the ball,
drops the bat,
and toddles away.
Run, run, I say,
and he waddles
around the yard,
laughing like a
babbling, bubbling,

quickly tumbling
brook,

and I remember.

His name is Huu Hein.
He followed me everywhere.
He follows me still,
and one day,
we're going
to find him.

≡

ACKNOWLEDGMENTS

I am grateful to the countless veterans, war correspondents, and photographers whose brave, unflinching recollections aided me in my research. Thanks to my editor, Tracy Mack, whose winding blue paths helped me find my way deeper into the story. Thanks also to her assistant, Abby Ranger, and to Marijka Kostiw for her beautiful cover design. Thanks to Steve Fraser for his encouragement and to Jodi Reamer for her support and guidance. Thanks also to Daniel Marotta, the finest baseball player I know, for his expertise and advice, and to Rosemary Marotta, who always listens to my stories and asks others to listen too. As always, I am most grateful to Marc, Celia, and Alex for their love and support.